the red wardrobe

To my Father

sarah corbett
the red wardrobe

seren

seren

is the book imprint of
Poetry Wales Press Ltd.
First Floor, 2 Wyndham Street
Bridgend, Wales, CF31 1EF

Cataloguing In Publication Data for this book
is available from the British Library

ISBN:1-85411-216-3

*The publisher acknowledges the financial assistance of the
Arts Council of Wales*

Cover Art: *Tree Pearl* by Simon Hicks

Printed by: WBC Book Manufacturers, Bridgend.

Contents

Easter

Your black eye is what comes,
its flick of light.
Then your brow, as broad
as the palm of my hand.

A long crack of bone severs
the dark, a door opened
on warmth; your nostrils
are lit coals fuming.

I have the smell of you,
of coming to life again,
the full forgotten sweetness
of flesh and dung;

sour earth spills into the room
as your great weight gains
the ground, shakes off death
like a shower of flies.

This is the power of returning:
the patterns we gather
like voices remembered in stone,
that mean always spring, a river.

I have called you —
the swing of your shoulder
is in my shoulder, in my hands,
the touch map of your skin.

Bark Find

I have returned: a girl of six or seven,
given to finding the edge of things —
a track ending in nettles,
a coppice of trees I dare not enter.

This is what calls me back —
a brace of afternoon light,
a shadow's imagined movement,
a leaf's fall long after the fall of winter,

and this: a husk of bark,
the inner bird of a tree
discarded and black-skinned,
a cat's sheared skin, one paw intact,

the day now
a dead thing, a cold burning.

Dream of a Horse

Rushes of breath in the dark —
at my face something is hot,
picking out pores in the skin.
Beneath my hands a belly heaves,
a trellis of veins steaming under silk.

A hoof strikes —
once, twice, the ground thundering.
A concurrence of tone and force
repeats through a puzzle of bone:
a long thigh against my hip, my breast to a
                                        sickle of rib.

It shifts balance, muscle clenched,
unclenched, remembering the taste of steel,
an insistence: at the mouth, hard at its flank —
the give and fold of neck,
the shoulder's force like water.

Around us, taking up the slack,
the air is sparse, sharp
to the sudden angle of an ear,
an eye rolling back its white
to catch sight of what it can smell.

Magpies

At this time of day
magpies gather in the branches,
a posse of thirty or so,
their black and white
sentinel against the sky.

A woman is framed
by the black bodies of trees.
She is stilled, momentary,
a slip, perhaps,
into some filmic memory.

Like me, she comes for this —
the shudder as the birds rise,
suddenly orchestral,
a thunder cloud
we count for its passing,

and how they leave us —
bare and expectant again
to the shadowless winter,
the intimacy of a lover's absence
drawing us in.

Ocyrhoe Becomes a Horse

She had not been content merely to learn her
father's arts, but could reveal in prophecy the
secrets of the fates.   — Ovid: Metamorphoses, Bk. 2

The words spoke themselves.
I heard my father's death
ring from my lips, foresaw my own fate
as if a great iron bell had uttered.

In the burn of the far hills
my maiden self is departing.
By the river where my mother
washed her hair and bore me, I am changing —

my flush skin becomes my bright hide,
my neck stretches towards the sun,
my hands push and harden.
The beast stirs, it paces in my blood,

my tongue thickens on consonants;
the wind, sharp in my throat,
carries the imprint of water,
the plain's constant notation.

I am lost, unhappy daughter,
who could see what she could not change,
to the fever that rankles in my bones,
the earth's thunder.

Blood Lines

There is something dangerous of you in me,
in the electricity my own veins generate,
in the shape my fist makes against the wall.
Here it is again, finding its voice,
as close to blood as I'll get.

You are washing my sister's hair in the sink,
the kitchen chair backed to the drainer.
Then someone comes through the door
and you are gone. Where you'd been,
the loud silence a slammed door leaves.

It's morning now. You're showing me
how your long legs cycle the sunlight,
how to hold a cigarette: two lips and two
                              fingers gesturing.
Where your wrap has fallen open
a nipple is pointing its rude head.

Roses

It was that summer — before Elvis died,
before we realized
how the climate might change things.
You, my cousin, were skimming the hedgerows
for Cabbage Whites,
making a cage of your fingers for their quick breath.

I collected Dog Roses,
their pink hearts fluttering in my fist.
Under my bed I had shut out summer,
each night learning the cool squares of the lino,
crushing the sheaves of the flower
until they bled their scent into the jar.

The house, enchanted under the astonishing sun,
hung out its linen like bright tongues,
heaving its faint osmosis
through open windows and doors,
frowsty with the fug of roses,
effused in their hot black rot for weeks.

Inventing My Mother

I invent you,
a conjuring trick with shadows.
Here you are, smelling of the night,
a halo of you,
tingling and darkly alive.

Here are your eyes,
their black centres mimic mine,
dead stars growing
in the sky's fabric;
the inverse of light.

Here are your hands,
an offering of fruits —
the mid-ness of things in an apple's skin,
the mayhem latent
in a fall of plums.

I have your name
but choose to keep it secret,
whispering its magic
to the mice in the walls,
their knowing smiles.

I have the touch
of your hand at my face,
waking me from a bad dream,
the memory of each finger's
cold kiss.

My Mother's Lover

My mother has a new lover.
He shovels the clutter from her head
like the coalman, heaps of hot stone
clattering beneath the house;
leaves before we awake.

She says he soothes her,
the palm of her right hand complaining
against the crook of her spine.
I imagine him smearing the heat of his olive skin
across her back, burning.

Last night she let me taste her lipstick,
tacky dabs of mauve on my mouth.
She talked of his fine hands,
the fingers with their bulbous tips,
how they make you shiver, electric.

I could see him, putting his finger
to her tongue, causing the lights
under the closed lids to jump and spark;
she showed me too how they kissed,
putting her electric tongue to mine and giggling.

The Red Wardrobe

The red wardrobe where you shut in my sister,
the iron key sliding into your pocket.

The red wardrobe that fell on my sister,
its colour old blood and rusty oil
on the soft blue insides of her elbows, her wrists,

like the Chinese burns she gave me
as I cried and hated her, until I remembered
how she made herself small in corners,
how I thought she was a kitten crying until I shook her.

The red wardrobe, its doors opening and closing in
                                        my dream,
the warm nuts in its dust becoming mice eyes,
their long tails, scratching,

that my father splintered and burnt
the day all the women left and we had fireworks.

Bitter Fruit

My mother is an impostor.
She is at her looking glass,
every day I hear her speak to it,
she says, "mirror, mirror..."

In the middle of the night
she is at my doorway,
a rain-cloud, a storm gathering.
Her fingers spark in the darkness.

I know she wants my heart,
she is jealous as a fish.
She would eat it,
a fat berry darkening her lips.

I will run away.
I will live in the forest
learning to run on my hands,
love the smell of foxes and their ways,

hole up like the beginning
of something — a pupa in a lace egg,
looking out at the world
from under a leaf.

If she finds me, I will change
into a pumpkin and poison her soup.
I will change into a mouse
and stampede all over her toes.

I will be a magnificent horse,
win prizes and be admired.
I will be a fairy princess,
wow everyone on the high wire with
                    my loop the loop.

And she will dance on coals
to show her appreciation.
She will cut off her toes
to fit in my shoes.

Ghost Mother

You are the fear
before sleeps comes, the claw
in the corner of the dark
that scratches at the boards.

You are the empty moon
full of the night, a question
with only questions
for answers.

You are a turned vowel,
the inside of a hole
that sings like the rubbed rim
of a glass.

You are a smudge of hair
in the bath, the ghost
of a mouth on a fold
of paper.

You are always present
in your absence —
a fragrant skin shed
in the hallway

into which I fall.

Shame

I have turned the tide from the shore,
watched the blue whale drown,
singing as he drifts to the sea bed.

I have listened a thousand times
to the pig, his throat's red shout
spilling an ambush of stars in the yard,

and I have seen the hanged woman,
swinging musically on her rope,
her hands, folded to a paper hat,

big jointed and thin as cuttlefish;
the scent memory of place
that lingers and will not show itself.

I know the exact angle of her face
in the dark, the butterfly wings of her shadow
flitting against the wall,

how she gave me a handful of shells
to pass the game of time with,
the ruined clicks of my heart.

And When Did You Last See Your Mother?

I'm always watching for her,
but all I remember is the curtain of her straight brown hair,
her owl's-face glasses.

This is my last memory.
It is a mountain I cannot shift or bring to me.
Its distance is her hands on my shoulders pushing me away.

Her round mouth fades out;
we are shouts in the wind, losing direction,
birds in a storm, rain coming in over a dark sea.

But like the first time, how can the last time be fixed —
was it that forced embrace as she walked away,
high square heels, hair brushing her back,

or do I meet her each morning,
shaking her limbs from her sleep,
stretching with her fingers and toes to touch me again?

Mornings

for Quest

It was when we rode out early
to chase the hares from their hollows
that I knew you most —

listening for my hands
as if you could trace each finger's suggestion
back to my heart's movement.

I would come, before I was expected,
and lie with you, my palms
to the hot undersides of your elbows

where the skin bags to pure silk
and I am at your beginning,
here, where we would nose and blink at the dawn,

waking to each other, learning the shape
of what is known and to be trusted.

Wood Sister

You have grown from the missed beat of my heart,
a slough of dry skin, a lost hair.

Your flesh is in my hands,
an envelope of you to be steamed and opened —

the long scar of your back, the bones of your feet,
the jut of hip holding its force.

I unfold your ears, where dirt moulds,
treasures to be snuffed out and eaten;

I can taste the dead wood of my dreams on you,
crawling from your splits and seams.

We earth here, this dark place is home.
Only the moon shows through the cracks in our skin.

Siamese

Sister, other half
of my heart, one is not enough

and I would die for you.
Life is a vision

in two matching halves,
there is no room between us

for disagreement.
The individual escapes us,

the other in me is the other in you;
a forked tongue speaks us,

we have many eyes and many ways to face.
We dream in tandem —

broad highways lined with oak trees
branching into the distance,

a curiosity of watermelon
joined at the root.

We fear a meeting at crossroads,
the anaesthesia

of bright lights, knives.
At night I listen

to the resonance
of your skin on my skin,

our shared nub of pleasure;
your breath slowing

into our one beat of sleep.
We hold hands across

the dual round of our world.
Alone cannot reach us here.

The Visit

I'm full of holes, she said.
I could see right through her.
Her holes were like finger holds,
I hooked her around my finger.

I knew I was dreaming her,
the sun begged at the curtain.
I held on, her soft mouth shedding leaf mould,
the sour scent of lavender.

She put out her hands,
she had bruises on her wrists
as if a dog had closed its kind teeth around them,
a bracelet of purple beads.

She lifted her dress,
showed me her popped button belly,
her bush growing flowers,
yellow clowns' blooms laughing.

Her seaweed hair streamed in my face,
she was a cunning fish
slipping quietly into the morning.

In the Asylum

Here, with the exact beauty
of a line of bright pills,

we have ordered our days
into daydreams. Each night

we resurrect ourselves,
the smell of us, dancing

in pools of light
from the corridor, earthing over

the daily anaesthetic.
From waste paper bins, toilet bowls,

we dig out our tongues,
send songs to imaginary planets

or lodge our stories, quietly,
under the skin.

By morning, we are ready to die
all over again.

Between the bars
and the panes of glass, our ghosts

are always at the window.
They follow us everywhere we go,

looking back
from their cold prison.

Peel the fingers from any fist,
if a hand

would warm in yours,
find the imprint of wings.

Changing

A woman stands in a walled garden,
her bare toes red on brown earth.
She gives nothing away,
her long face turned to the bitter wind.

Her hair is loose, her dress mimics her limbs.
She is lean as the cold day,
the rooks that gather around her
for what might fall, unspoken, from her hands.

She is watching for the light to shift its grey,
the darkness promised in the stone of the wall.
She is empty and could journey beyond this place,
lifting off like a bird's shadow.

But she remains, rooted and reaching.
I can feel the tender bark of her thighs,
the moisture seeping into her veins,
the tight buds that still themselves under the skin.

Bird Man

He wants to be a bird.
It's in his rib's hollow pot,

his hip's shimmy at the window.
He is wandering over the rooftops,

watching for where the houses
edge out to brown fields,

where the branches sway
to the pink of the sky.

He is wondering how his belly
tips and curves to the earth,

is a whistling, singing bowl,
about the way of the wind,

how it lifts then licks his bones,
filters through to his skin's core.

If I held him, he would pass
like feathers from my hands,

he is as light as that —
two words might carry him.

Here we are, circling.
We paint breathless maps,

our fingers flap at the glass.

Sleepless

For Ruairi

Morning is wakeful, 8 am and watchful,
morning is here, we are close to touching it;
this is its movement: your hand, your hip.

At noon we can say what we like,
it is a pigeon, it coos and permits everything.
Then your tongue at my lips.

The afternoon begins here, a new chicken.
It is in our palms, ready — we listen:
4 o'clock, your signature, opening.

8 pm and we still haven't eaten.
You are at the window, fingering the evening,
it sets us down lightly, its plumage.

This is midnight — crumpled, salt-worn,
a sea without fish and moonless;
zero-time, skip-time, ours.

It is 4 am, we know this:
the chair has a smile now, the curtains are singing —
morning approaches despite us.

Letter to a Lover

I am sending you my heart,
it will be my messenger,
a hummingbird singing at a flower.

Isn't this beautiful, what you have of me?
Does it still beat against its sides,
is it breathless?

Does it hold its colour —
of my night-long forays under the skin,
the inside burgundy of tulips?

It is a beetle, armoured and glistening.
If you put your finger to it
it will split and spread wings.

An impatient creature,
it has guessed that you think of me,
the ridge of my hip, my belly's henge.

Here I am, a nail
finding its place under my breast,
a slate of bone prised into my palm.

The Quarrel

This sharp tongue
is the true mechanism
of my heart.
You have to be quick
to miss it.

There's a knack
to keeping me sweet:
climb into my anger,
and, once there,
touch me.

After the women
of a certain African tribe —
in the shaved arch
of their pubis
each clitoris a swallow's egg —

I carry my intentions
before me;
you may choose to look
or turn away.

Morning Interiors

To live in a house
I may have lived in years ago
and returned to by chance, as in a dream,
rediscovered and alive again —

inventing the scene from a window
at the end of a staircase,
rooms you can only guess at the darkness they hold
from the cracks in the stonework —

like the house near Malham,
where I could have lived, cooling the butter
under the eaves of the end-barn,
tracing the pungent hoof-falls of cattle before dawn,

where I put my face and palm to a scrape of plaster
and smelt the nettles rising through the walls,
certain of the power to heal and warn
that comes with this listening.

Waking again to this unowned yet familiar place,
where a cup or the light behind a blind will slowly
                                        name itself,
I wonder where I might have been or could be —
shaping the scroll on a fireplace,

the angle of the shoulder turned against mine —
and slip back into my boat of sleep,
its insistent, insistent motion.

Drowning

I took the sun with me, travelled her light.
My cotton dress lifted gracefully,
slipped like oil from my wrists.

I remember the surprise of your face,
how it blurred into the sky,
the water closing its soft hoop
over my head,

and knew, as the river found my bones,
pushed its intangible weight
under my skin,

that you still waited at the prow
of our boat, watching for the sea,
words soundless on the back of your tongue,

the waves, as you passed, parting
and coming together again.

In the House That We Built

To enter, first
say its name, then shoulder
the door, hitch up its low hinges.
It still scrapes the stone flags

as it opens. Once inside, note
the whisper of moss in its stone,
the constant tap of earth
under the floor, how little light

passes the glare of the window.
It was never ours,
we were always an exchange in darkness,
intruders hiding our noise

in its walls. Windows, nailed
in their new frames, never quite
opened right, and try as we might
we could not silence the rafters,

their squabbling after hours
as if our dreams confused them.
The clotted orchard gave us
its fruit, apple foetus in-turned

and damaged, plums that bit us.
Its garden's grasses sliced
our fingers, harboured stinging nettles,
small beasts that increased

the pulse. I remember you, sweeping
and sweeping the outhouse floor,
the dust coming again as thick
as snow, your eyelids rimed with it,

your knuckles whitening at the broom;
you, bright suddenly in a brace of sun,
shifting layers like years, unable
to reach the clear floor of things.

Skin

These nights I'm gathering
reeds from the riverbed.
The outward memory of things,
they hang and sing at my fire.

Once, I lost a child.
She had no surfaces,
took up no space to speak of,
but in slipping, slipped into this —

the detail of washing my hair
at the sink, and slowly,
my hands circling the scalp,
the brute pull of her blood.

A beached dog stinks in the sun —
sea debris, a heap of skin.
She, too, returns, her hung teats,
the boat of her belly.

Messenger, with her silent
show of teeth, she asks nothing of us.
I hitch my skirts and wait
for the dark water to take me in.

Ghosts

Far safer through an Abbey gallop,
The stones achase,
Than, moonless, one's own self encounter
In lonesome place.

Ourself, behind ourself concealed
Should startle most;...
                    Emily Dickinson - 'Ghosts'

I
At Skipton Castle

Perhaps it was that train in the night
that brought you to this place,
a towering wall built into rock,
the rush of the river
under its floating epaulettes of ice.

Like emerging from a dream
into the day before yesterday,
the exaggerated familiarity
of the woman in the post office
and what she will say next,

and then the slow realization,
as if you're waking from a long sleep,
upside down in your bed, shock to the wall,
that where you've come back to
is where you've been before:

the courtyard with its central oak
planted on your mother's wedding day,
and where you watch from your room,
a handprint lifting off from the window
and becoming your fist.

II
Tŷ Gwyn

Gwernymynydd, North Wales

Is this a haunting,
or is it some trick of memory
that brings them here,
bumping up against you on the Queen Anne sofa,
mouthing wet O's of mist in hallway mirrors
as you pause to check its image against your own?

It is as if someone had got here before you
and was now hiding
in the lining of another house,
stitched into the paperings and re-matched linen,
having stored something of themselves, like witch
blessings,
in the scratches under the lintel of the fireplace.

The woman who lives here —
a house that reclaims you, brings you back —
tells how they once slammed doors,
clambered noisily, like uninvited whores, under
her sheets,
how, having pledged a slice of herself,
a cache of blood within the walls,
they have retreated,

lingering softly in the dust
in a brace of light on the stairwell,
in lavender suddenly scenting a room as you leave.

III
The House on First Avenue

There was the time in Devon
when the inscription on the wall of our cottage
spoke to me, and drew in my hand.
Its words made waves in the evening light
like heat rising off new tarmac.
I carried a bruise on my forehead all week,
an extra lightness to my shoulder
as if something cold had just lifted.

At home, in the house on First Avenue,
ghosts left their faces,
abandoned behind curtains in the dark
or an unexpectedly closed door,
where sometimes only a trace of it lingered:
a certain thickening of the atmosphere,
how you know who's been in your room
by the thumbprint they leave on the air.

If I turned back, leaving the house,
there would be one of them
staring out from the window:
a parody of Munch, a bald surprise,
an indiscernible presence in the background,
barely recognizable, yet a reminder still
that something of me was always waiting
in the room where I'd left it.

Meeting the Alien

It was December, the night
an offering, winter's creature
unfolding its warmed belly,
its eye's dark dream.

I was in-between, a blindness
of moons when anything can happen,
walking into the wind, opening
as a leaf opens to rain.

You could say an angel came,
a blaze of unnamed light hitting me.
I swear I was taken, touched
on inside places, beyond the skin.

Perhaps they were gods,
they did not resemble us.
They were music resonating
a power like horses, like newborn things.

They left me half-naked in the freezing river.
On the bank the blank trees
were uncalled spirits
and far off the hills were waking.

Now, I chart the shifting
points of light, the shock of dark,
wonder what it is of me
that spins in their universe,

listen in with the stars
to learn the tapestry of myself
I had never known,
the wide night that we share.

The Housewife's Tale

A clean slice of morning
paints itself across the dresser.
I wipe and wipe until the day removes it.

I shower for the first time, then again,
after the postman has delivered his dirty letters.
Overnight, the kitchen has soiled itself.

My children catch in this ritual web;
we touch and wash, watch the residues of love
spiral down the shiny round of the plughole.

When I was five, a visiting uncle
lifted the crinked pleat of my dress,
ran a finger along the inside hem of my pants.

He said, *this is a sweet and secret thing,*
keep it for me. If you tell the world
will burn and fall from its axis. It hurts there still.

I rinse each egg before boiling it,
carefully peel and throw away the shell,
deal out the plates, individually wrapped and safe.

In the cunning light of the fridge
I chart the multiplication of enzymes,
an army facing it out over the bacon.

At night and under cover, he comes closer,
my husband, he who so kindly holds me
as I shake out my contaminated tears.

We love in different tongues,
take turns in a salt bath.
When he sleeps, I imagine the world pure.

The Flower Garden

They drank tea from china cups
as if nothing could touch them,
warm buns buttering their fingers.

After lunch my grandmother
would lead them along a row of blooms,
nestling in their bed

or shouting themselves out of it —
each head of colour rude against the other,
their long stems rubbing.

In a feathery palm she would cup
the velvet tube of a lily,
watch the sun bounce on white skin,

or, inviting a friend closer,
pull back the folds of a rose
to reveal its scent.

At night, window open to her garden,
I hope she dreamt
of cool leaves against her belly,

petals, damp from the night dew,
stroking her cheek,
the lips of the rose returning.

The Bee King

In the woods I saw him,
he smelt of the honey season,
dead flower water

and hummed loudly
a swarming song;
its pattern coiled you in.

He danced, stamped in a circle
a map of himself,
slapped time at his side

as the black coat flapped,
flashed his yellow breast,
his ready sting in his fist.

Running, I thought of the orchid
who fools the bee,
puts out her bee-like vulva,

and, as her lover
humps in vain, powders
him with her seed.

When I returned, he'd left
his name in ashes,
his battered crown,

a honeycomb of juice in the grass.

The Bread Thief

He is big as a house
in the shoulder, four-square,
gifted with his tongue
at a salt palm; red

as a fox in the sun,
bold in the unblink
of his eye — a black olive
of an eye, fluted

like a queen's. He has
the trick to the catch
of the door, his lips soft
at the latch, an undoer

of knots and strategies,
at ease with the subterfuge
of an afternoon,
the pleasure of owning

another's absence.
In the pantry the new
bread waits, swollen,
expectant for the cut

grass of his breath, his black
nostril steaming at the bin.
Here he is, he noses
in, insistent, wet

for the taste of what
is fragrant and forbidden;
the hedge a torn letter,
his hooves half moons in the lawn.

Catherine the Great's Horse

According to rumour, Catherine the Great, in consequence of her
exotic and excessive desires, met her fate when a horse fell as it was
being lowered, via slings and pulleys, into her.

This groom is a good man,
I trust in the scent of his breeches,
the straw in his heart.

Each morning he massages me
until my skin is burnished silver.
Shoulder to my shoulder
he oils my hard round hooves.

They bring the mare,
her tease tipping his nose
under her cocked tail, her ready scent
staining the inside of her thighs.

I call softly to her,
eyeing the conker brown haunches
as they wrinkle and tense,
her fat dark vulva winking,

mount, bite the base of her neck,
embrace the slope of her shoulder,
the groom's cool palm on my sex
guiding me in.

All I know is her ribbed inside,
muscle meeting muscle
and the taste of her rising on my tongue.
We cum to the pulse of our world,
hearts heaving in our bellies.

Below the gilded halls
the courtiers check then double check
the stitching, put their weight against the ropes,
grease the coils and turns of the winch.

The groom arrives early,
hands nervous with my straps.
Today, we're in the service of the queen, he says.
That goodly, strange queen.

Heloise to Her Lover

For Susan Wicks, because she dreamed it.

Not wife; do I darn your sleeves,
night by night fraying
my eyes at the cuffs
in the raw scrub of a kitchen?

Call me mistress and we'll dance
with wine in our hands
as stars extinguish themselves
on our naked shoulders.

Or better, whore, and we'll watch
ourselves grow against the wall,
play at making animals in the candlelight,
their noises in the fold of my tongue,

your two fingers
a frightened rabbit inside me.

Jocasta

I should have known it was him,
the violet flicker of his eyes was mine,
the years tied in.

Shaving, making coffee,
he sang like a hot samovar
a sudden lyric I found familiar.

His neat prick fitted me, burned there,
each night was a returning
I could never fathom.

Oh, he was a swan,
he grew into me,
his blond plumage darkening.

We made a river of ourselves,
filtering out through mauve dawns
while the land bled.

We were faultless, riddles caught us.
Our child ran with us,
was whole, a happy oracle.

Now we are shattered leaves.
Here, I slip the rope,
his eyes thicken the dust.

Athena

I sprang from my father's brow,
his twin-eyed surprise.

When he found me, squat in his palm,
he named me for a great city, war.

As a girl I wanted nothing
but the straight side of a triangle,

to catch a serpent and wring
the wisdom from its patterned skin.

They say an image of me fell from the sky,
lit the broad seas golden,

they say many things: that I breathe storms,
gather in the wind.

But I am more than this —
I am all of you and nothing less.

In my bones my father rages:
Thunder-Master, War-Brute, God of Gods;

in my blood my mother:
unnamed, unspoken, a beautiful zero;

on my shield I carry a serpented head,
it stares like stone into the future. Sings.

Venus on Her Birthday

This is my big day.
Here I am, blushing,
a sherbet and cream harlot
blown in on a seashell.

Have I missed something,
cold as alabaster as I am?
I crave a muscular warmth,
a hand reaching out, sighing.

Instead, it's raining roses,
their wet scent staining the light.
They are bloodless, washed out versions,
a silence for shouting.

On the shore a man paints.
With his brush poised he waits, waits.

Still Life with Pears

Those pears, so pleased with themselves,
full bellied sultans and blushing.
They are certain of their weight,
how they represent light
stilled in one place, and,
holding the tone of their daubed colours,
will not be eaten.

The grapes, on the other hand,
are unfinished.
They slip into brown, forgetful of their purpose.
Uncalled, half-lost children,
they are dream walkers,
making night music with the dark corners.

The apples and the red jug
are eating the shadows.
They shout against the chequered cloth
how a paintbrush is a dumb thing.
Rounding into their angles
like boxed cattle, they stare out, as if it were us
being rude in looking.

Dark Moon

This is the dark me —
twisted body of a hawthorn,
the latent witching of that tree,
its black muscle harming itself
but growing old, an ugly face
proud to be ugly,
a sneer at beautiful things.

Prepare yourself,
I may bud and burst —
a veiled hag, a trick of spring
that watches inwards, turns
and turns a hallowed magic
from my harsh skin,
my spiked and flowering hands.

Night Flying

I always kick off from the grass,
cruise out over the estuary,
the salt marshes blue and silver
under the moon,

a night heron
sparking for the ghost of fish,
a slough of wind under my wings,
the gasp of winter

in my throat
as I track the sea's edge
breaking its eggs at the shore.
I could as soon

fold into the low land —
the shadow grasses,
the sudden pools of myself —
its soft push dark in me,

or lift again, return
to roof-slope, gutterings,
the black-out of a window
slowly opening, becoming a face.

The Electric Dead

We are like flies,
living on nothing but air.

We sit for long hours in the grass
to watch beetles roll their eggs

along the stems of flowers,
observe how trees bud

then shed their leaves in colours,
shattering the sunlight;

how any face will fracture
into a thousand shining points

if you look in the right way.
We believe that travelling through time

is only a matter of will,
and that in time

we will have stopped for long enough
to see the centuries through again.

Our moons sit with the sun,
we are guided by the stories the stars suggest;

we are always dreaming,
but do not distinguish

between what is felt and what is imagined.

Pylons

In the fields beyond the town
the pylons have wings. They grew in the night,
cocooned then flowered.
From our beds we listened
to the steel-edged moans of their making.

Now we have gathered,
a carnival crowd drawn
by the snap and whiplash of lines.
We watch as they heave to the sun,
flock in the sky and darken us.

Yet we are hopeful for them,
we send them our children's names
as if it was us that set them loose,
and, in doing so, wonder where they will land
and who will find them.

Nearly gone, they flash,
quick lit tapers burning out
in the last of the day's light,
their scattered messages falling
as soft rain on upturned faces.

Tunnels

For Esther, and anyone who's ever been on a road protest.

If you make the right sounds you will be heard,
your concerns will be returned, redoubled in consequence.

It's like beeping your horn in tunnels
and waiting for the response —

the retort above the engine hum coming back to you,
finding a life of its own in a lost rhythm — jazz and laughter,

a rear window explosive under a child's hand.
Remember — all the roads we build and leave behind us

will be reclaimed, returned to roots again and flowers;
and again, you know that behind each wheel and mirror,

in every blind tunnel,
we can shout into the dark and be answered.

Dig

We'd dug hard for days,
fingering the soil like rich wives testing silk
or monks with parchment,
ready for the glint, incised edge,
an odd smoothness to a stone;
each shouldering a part of the sun,
squat beneath the blind sky.

And every night we returned
to that hill, its sub-terrain
etching out its landscape in our dreams,
dug under, scrabbling at the turf and grit
with our bare hands, blood
bubbling up from our fingertips
like rare beads of glass;

entering as children enter the dark:
skin alive, holding hands,
the iron smell of wet earth
worming into our bellies, echoing there.

Communion

Last night you called,
your red brush sparks of stars.
I saw you slip into shadow,
glance back, your red eyes hold,

followed you here, nested
on curled bark, skeletons,
the blood of your lips, your stink,
your cheek's clotted fur.

Earthed, rolled into this root place,
we dreamed of the hunt —
the quick warmth of wide-eyed things
against the earth's cold spine,

the jive of a hare's bones
under its sheath of skin.

Wintering

We are hidden things,
backs hardened with the dark,
starved on leaf-mould, the year's leavings,
the black filigree of winter.

We wait, laying up time
under the soil's crust,
listen to the night let down its leaves,
the moon crackle in its glass,

pressing our faces
to the frosted roots of the world
to tongue its latent whiteness,
its hidden store of warmth.

This is our home —
the long months,
the thin sun in a sharp sky,
the web of twilight.

Here, we dream as quietly as birds.
Seeds split and uncurl about us,
rising from the ground
to the earth's light.

Pilgrims

We are shedding our country,
it splits and falls away,
indifferent as parchment.
Cliffs signal to the continent
how no blunt fingers
have scrabbled their features.

Behind us, the beach
is a lone figure listening to our absence,
the owl-call of the wind
knocking the lantern from its hand,
the sea shifting relentlessly
against its shoulder.

Out here, we are blind children
touching water, our hands trailing
in the suddenness of the past.
Kinship dies on the tongue,
its tasted grain shared, diminished,
now a remembered thing.

We are lost, drifting into the dark;
at our backs night folds its hands.

Fishermen

We can smell the wind,
it weaves into our shoreline,
patterning our hand's movement, our dreams.

The tug of the current
mimics our wives' turnings —
we are womaned in the circle of a day.

In our boat a heart beats —
we ride in the hands of the beast,
feed it the sea's salt givings.

Backs to the village, where lights
flick their tails and our children drift,
their sleepy eyes hungry,

we glisten, silvered in the dawn,
slip back and down to the coral.

Watermark

We had not yet reached the sea.
We heard nothing of it, not a whisper in the distance,
not a hint, far off, of its music,
not even the smell of sex in its beds.
There was only its blue, the source of blue,
stretched across the horizon.

Overnight, a daffodil found its colour.
We could not imagine our destination,
only the first face of this flower, its yellow certain.
We walked for hours, made love as an old man watched,
thinking we had not seen him,
slept fitfully in the deep shingle as the day hit us,
touched nothing the sun hadn't touched;

warm as pebbles, bright and big as the sky
spreading us wide in its wide arms
like two seabirds sighting the land's end.
And still, the sea's question —
a handful of shells finding their way back to us —
when will you come?

Acknowledgements

Acknowledgements are due to the following magazines and anthologies where some of these poems first appeared: *Scratch, Iron,Poetry London Newsletter, Poetry Review, Poetry Wales, Stand Magazine, Envoi, The Rialto, Agenda* (Anthology of New Poems, 1998), *Orbis*.

I would like to thank the Society of Authors for an Eric Gregory Award.